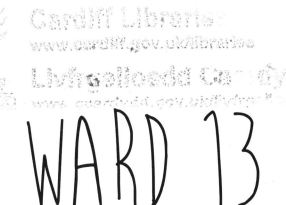
WARD 13

Titles in Teen Reads:

BILLY BUTTON
CAVAN SCOTT

DAWN OF THE DAVES
TIM COLLINS

DEAD SCARED
TOMMY DONBAVAND

DEADLY MISSION
MARK WRIGHT

FAIR GAME
ALAN DURANT

JIGSAW LADY
TONY LEE

HOME
TOMMY DONBAVAND

KIDNAP
TOMMY DONBAVAND

MAMA BARKFINGERS
CAVAN SCOTT

PEST CONTROL
CAVAN SCOTT

SITTING TARGET
JOHN TOWNSEND

STALKER
TONY LEE

THE HUNTED
CAVAN SCOTT

THE CORRIDOR
MARK WRIGHT

TROLL
TIM COLLINS

UNDERWORLD
SIMON CHESHIRE

WARD 13
TOMMY DONBAVAND

WORLD WITHOUT WORDS
JONNY ZUCKER

Badger Publishing Limited, Oldmedow Road, Hardwick Industrial Estate, King's Lynn PE30 4JJ
Telephone: 01438 791037

www.badgerlearning.co.uk

WARD 13

TOMMY DONBAVAND

Badger LEARNING

Ward 13 ISBN 978-1-78147-799-1

Text © Tommy Donbavand 2014
Complete work © Badger Publishing Limited 2014

Publisher: Susan Ross
Senior Editor: Danny Pearson
Publishing Assistant: Claire Morgan
Copyeditor: Cheryl Lanyon
Designer: Bigtop Design Ltd

2 4 6 8 10 9 7 5 3 1

CHAPTER 1

THE LONER

Squeak. Squeak. Squeak.

Mark Jackson pulled himself higher against his pillows, all thoughts of achieving the high score on his skateboarding game lost.

The bed was coming back.

He winced as a dagger of pain shot through the break in his tibia. His science teacher would have been proud to discover that he knew the name of at least one of the bones in his leg – even if it had taken a skate park accident, a plaster cast and now an impending operation for him to learn it.

Squeak. Squeak. Squeak.

Mark glanced around the faces of his fellow patients in Ward 13. Why weren't they paying attention? Surely they could all hear the squeaking wheel of the bed as it came closer. Surely they had begun to notice the same pattern he had…

He caught two of the nurses – the one with the curly hair and the one called Helen – sharing a nervous glance. They knew – he was certain of that. That's why he could never get a straight answer out of either of them.

How long had the bed been away? Mark grabbed his PS Vita, closed the game and checked the time. 5.40pm. Almost dinner time. That meant the bed had left the ward just over four hours ago. Four hours. Was that how long it took to complete a hernia operation? Who knew?

SQUEAK. SQUEAK. SQUEAK.

Mark could hear the porter's shuffling footsteps accompanying the dodgy wheel. The bed was almost here. The bed that, when it had left the ward not long after lunchtime, had contained a patient. An older guy, called Jack. The guy who was suffering with a hernia. The guy who didn't have any family to visit him when the doors to Ward 13 were opened to the public every night.

Jack had been the ringleader of the group he jokingly called 'The Loners'. He had been the one to notice that Mark also sat alone during visiting hours, his head buried in his video game. On Mark's third evening, he had limped across the ward to join him.

"Visiting time again, huh?"

Mark had nodded, barely looking up from his game.

Jack hadn't been put off. "You expecting anyone tonight? Mum, or dad?"

Mark had shaken his head. "Don't have parents."

"Oh, I'm sorry…"

"Don't be," said Mark, looking up at Jack properly for the first time. He glanced at the Royal Navy tattoo on the man's forearm. "I'm not sorry. You don't miss what you've never had."

"I guess not," Jack had said. "No other family, then?"

Another shake of the head. "I live in Keating House."

"The children's home? Down by the High Street?"

"Yep."

"But you must have carers there?"

Mark had nodded. "They can't leave the other kids to come and sit with me, though. We're short-staffed most of the time."

"The other kids? Your friends…"

"Not allowed out after six o'clock – but I'm playing one of them online right now. His name's Liam."

"Well, I guess that's as good as having a visitor," Jack had smiled. Then, he'd pushed himself to his feet and started to limp back in the direction of his own bed.

BEEP. Mark had paused the game. "What about you?"

Jack had paused and turned. "Me? No. No one. There was my sister, Elsie – but she's been gone a while now."

Mark had waved the handheld console in Jack's direction and grinned. "I'll tell Liam you said hello."

"You do that!"

SQUEAK! SQUEAK! SQUEAK!

Mark could see the shadow of the bed as it approached the entrance to the ward. Just a few hours earlier, Jack had waved groggily to him as he'd been wheeled away for his operation. Now Mark would know whether his suspicions were true, or if he was imagining everything. He screwed his eyes shut and crossed his fingers tightly. *Please please please please please please…*

The porter's hands trembled as he turned the bed into Ward 13 and slowly pushed it back to its spot by the far wall.

Mark waited until he could hear the bed passing the end of his, then he forced himself to open his eyes and look.

His skin turned cold.

The bed was empty.

Jack was gone.

CHAPTER 2

THE LIES

"Nurse!"

Mark stabbed repeatedly at the button on his buzzer. Where were all the nurses? This was supposed to be a hospital. What if he had fallen out of bed, or something? Didn't there have to be someone around at all times?

"Nurse!"

Some of the other patients were looking at him now, over the tops of paperback books or around the pages of their newspapers. Mark almost screamed in frustration. Why were they looking at him when they should have been looking at the empty bed? At Jack's bed!

Eventually, the nurse with the curly hair came hurrying into the ward. "What's the matter, Mark?" she asked, a smile fixed in place. "Got another itch under your cast?"

Mark ignored her question. "Where's Jack?" he demanded. He saw a flash of something behind the nurse's eyes. Anger? Fear? Whatever it was, it was gone as quickly as it had arrived.

The nurse tutted. "Look at the state of your pillows," she said, pulling Mark upright so that she could rearrange the bedding behind him. "It's no wonder you can't sleep at night if you're losing half your pillows."

Mark pushed himself back and stared straight at the nurse. "Where is Jack?"

"Oh, I don't know," said the nurse, avoiding his gaze. "I imagine he's gone home."

"Home?" repeated Mark. "He's gone home from his hernia operation?"

"People do go home, you know," snapped the nurse. Now she was busying herself with Mark's sheets. "You will, too – once you've had your op on your leg."

"How did Jack go home?"

"What's that, now?"

Mark caught the nurse's arm with his hand. She stopped fussing with his bedding and looked down at him. It may have been Mark's imagination, but he thought he could feel her trembling.

"How did Jack go home?"

"I expect one of his family came to collect him," replied the nurse.

Mark shook his head. "He doesn't have a family. Not since his sister died."

The nurse gently pulled her arm from Mark's grasp. "That's a shame." She turned to leave.

"None of them had families."

The nurse froze. She didn't turn back, but Mark could tell she was listening.

"Since I've been here, eight patients have been taken down from this ward for their operations. Three of them didn't come back. None of those three had family or friends come to visit them in the evenings. They had no one to miss them if they disappeared."

The telephone began to ring at the nurse's station in the corridor outside.

"I'd better get that," said the nurse, scurrying away.

Mark settled back against his freshly plumped pillows and watched the porter gather together Jack's belongings from the locker beside the

now-empty bed. His slippers, glasses case, half a bag of wine gums, a copy of the novel *Jaws*… He stuffed the items into a black bin liner, then scurried away, eyes nervously darting left and right.

The games console began to PING! repeatedly on the bed beside Mark. He picked it up and studied the screen. It was Liam, demanding a rematch for the high score on the skateboarding game.

Mark tapped 'ACCEPT' and began to play. The game would be fun, but not the same as having someone come in to sit beside his bed and talk during visiting hours. Like the other Loners, Mark had no one to miss him if he disappeared.

And his operation was set for first thing the following morning.

CHAPTER 3

THE KID

Dinner was disgusting. Worse than the spaghetti bolognese they'd served up the night before.

"Come on, son!" grinned the kitchen attendant through broken teeth. "Get it down you. It'll do you good!"

Mark ran his fork through the soggy mashed potatoes on the plate. They looked horrible enough – and the carrots were as hard as rocks – but it was the chicken breast that really looked as though it had seen better days. And… if Mark peered closely… he could almost make out some

sort of faint writing on the top of the piece of meat. He could make out a few letters … R… O… Y… A…

"You're not eating that!" said a voice, and the plate was snatched from his hands.

Mark looked up. The other nurse on duty that night – the one he'd heard others call Helen – was standing beside his bed.

"But, I'm hungry," Mark moaned. And he was. Even if the food didn't exactly look appetising, he hadn't had a bite to eat since the limp cheese sandwich he'd been given at lunchtime.

"Well, hospital food is no good for a growing young boy at the best of times!" said Helen, sliding the plate onto the bedside table. She reached into a bag at her side and pulled out a plastic tub. "I just had to wait until old Grotbags from the kitchen had gone before I could say so."

Mark took the tub and opened it. Inside was a large portion of lasagne – and it was still warm.

He looked up at the nurse.

"Leftovers from my dinner before I came on shift," she said. "But don't tell anyone else, or they'll all expect the same treatment." With that, she ruffled Mark's hair and hurried away.

Mark rested back against his pillows and grabbed the fork from the white goo pretending to be potatoes on the plate beside the bed. He took a mouthful of lasagne – delicious! Quickly, he began to tuck in.

That's when he noticed Archie in the far corner of the ward. Another member of Jack's Loners group, Archie was only nine years old. He was in Ward 13 waiting for an eye operation, and had a large white patch secured over the offending eye. Right now, he was peering suspiciously at his chicken with the good one.

Mark glanced down at the slab of lasagne in his tub and sighed. Sometimes it didn't pay to be the good guy. He pressed the lid back into place,

carefully climbed out of bed, and half hopped, half limped across the ward to Archie.

"Budge up!" he said, dropping onto the bed beside the younger boy.

Archie sniffed at the air. "What's in there?" he asked, eyeing the plastic tub.

"Lasagne," Mark replied. "Enough for both of us."

Archie dumped his hospital meal and both boys tucked into the home-prepared Italian food.

"This is great!" said Archie through a big mouthful.

Mark grinned. The kid was right. It was.

"My nan used to make lasagne like this," Archie said. "You know, before she…"

The pair fell quiet, but kept eating.

"Jack says it won't be too long before a foster family chooses me," said Archie. "He told me after we'd finished playing cards this morning."

Mark glanced along the line of beds on this side of the ward to the empty slot where Jack should have been. He carefully put down his fork.

"Archie…" he began, but he didn't have a chance to say any more. A cry came up from the nurse's station in the corridor outside.

"Dr Stone is coming!"

CHAPTER 4

THE SURGEON

Ward 13 flew into a panic. Half a dozen nurses appeared – including several Mark had never seen before – and they began to tidy up the room as quickly as they could.

Nurse Helen dashed over to Archie's bed and took Mark by the arm. "Come on," she said. "Time to get you back in your own bed."

"But we haven't finished eating…"

"Never mind that!" snapped the nurse. "Dr Stone expects everything to be in order for one of his visits."

"Who's Dr Stone?" asked Archie, shovelling as much of the remaining lasagne into his mouth as he could before the tub was taken away.

"His name is on the chart at the end of my bed," said Mark. "He's the surgeon who's doing the operation on my leg tomorrow." Suddenly, a thought struck him. "He's the surgeon doing all these operations, isn't he?"

But Nurse Helen didn't reply. She simply helped Mark hop back across Ward 13 and quickly tucked him back into his own bed.

Within a few minutes, the ward was as tidy as could be expected. The nurses lined up at the door, fussing with their uniforms, as a short man with thinning hair entered. He wore a long, white coat, and peered over the top of his glasses with cold, grey eyes.

He paused in the doorway of Ward 13 and looked around, taking everything in. "Good… Good…" he said. He smiled, but it was a movement of the mouth only. His eyes remained as emotionless as before.

Dr Stone strode into the ward as though he owned the place. "I hope you all enjoyed your dinner this evening!" he said loudly.

There was a vague mumble of a reply from the patients around the room.

"I said, I hope you all enjoyed your dinner this evening!"

A weak chorus of, "Yes, thank you" rang out.

"Good… Good…" He turned to the nurse with the curly hair. "Now, where is my first assignment for the morning?" he asked. "A Mr Jackson…"

Curly-hair exchanged another glance with Helen, then she led Dr Stone towards Mark's bed. "This way, Dr Stone."

The surgeon stopped at the foot of Mark's bed and snatched up the clipboard containing his notes. "Hmmm… a skateboarding accident I see, Mr Jackson."

Mark nodded. "I was trying to perform a daydream flip."

Dr Stone stared at him over his glasses. "A daydream flip?"

"It's a skateboard trick," said Mark. "But I got the landing wrong."

"You most certainly did," said Dr Stone. There was that cold smile again. "Two pins in your tibia tomorrow morning to hold the bone in place while it heals. Boys will be boys! I imagine your parents are horrified at what has happened."

The curly-haired nurse turned away and stared at the floor.

But Mark didn't look away, didn't break eye contact with Dr Stone. "I don't have parents," he said flatly. "No family at all, in fact. But then, I think you knew that."

"Well, isn't that a shame," said the surgeon, ignoring the comment. He replaced the clipboard at the end of Mark's bed and turned to leave.

"None of them had family," said Mark.

Dr Stone stopped, but didn't turn back. "Excuse me?"

"The patients who don't come back from your operating theatre," Mark continued. "None of them has a family to miss them."

Now Dr Stone did turn around, his grey eyes burning into Mark's like frozen lasers. "And why would you say something like that?"

Mark smiled and shrugged as innocently as he could. "Boys will be boys, I guess."

Without another word, Dr Stone span round and marched out of Ward 13. The patients and nurses finally allowed themselves to breathe again. Slowly, sounds of life began to return.

Mark slumped back against his pillows and stared at Jack's empty bed. He wouldn't have admitted it to anyone if they'd asked, but he was terrified.

CHAPTER 5

THE TRUTH

"Mark! Mark! Wake up!"

Mark opened his eyes and found the room in darkness. He'd been deep in a dream where he was the only patient left on Ward 13. Even the nurses had gone. He sat up groggily and squinted at the other beds in the dim light, relieved to find them still occupied.

"Mark, it's me!" hissed a voice.

Mark turned to find a small figure crouching at the side of his bed. "Archie! What do you want?"

"I want to talk," Archie replied. "I've noticed it, too."

"Noticed what?"

"That some people aren't coming back from their operations."

Mark sighed. "Archie, listen…"

"No!" Archie said firmly. "Don't tell me I'm making it up. I know you've already worked it out. I could tell by the way you talked to Dr Stone earlier."

"I could be wrong…"

"You're not," insisted Archie, "and don't try to fob me off because I'm just a kid. We're both due for our operations tomorrow and if we don't do something now, neither of us will be coming back."

Reluctantly, Mark nodded. "So, what do we do?"

"I think you were right to accuse Dr Stone of being involved in all this," said Archie. "We have to find out what he's up to."

"That's exactly what I was thinking," said Mark. "But I can hardly go wandering around the hospital at night with a broken leg."

Archie thought for a moment, then whispered, "Stay here…"

Mark watched as the young boy disappeared into the darkness, his bare feet slapping against the hard floor.

Ten minutes later, Archie was back – and he was pushing a wheelchair. "Your transport awaits!"

"Where did you get that?" asked Mark, pulling back his bed sheets.

"The store cupboard at the end of the corridor," Archie replied. "It wasn't locked."

"Just as well," said Mark.

"Yeah," agreed Archie. "It would have taken ages for me to pick the lock with just one eye…"

Shaking his head and smiling, Mark climbed into the wheelchair and allowed Archie to push him to the ward's exit. They stopped in the shadows – two nurses were sitting at the station, just outside.

"They weren't there a few minutes ago!" moaned Archie.

"Probably away somewhere checking on a patient," said Mark. "There are loads of single rooms down the far end."

"A patient?" whispered Archie. "Great idea…" Then he was gone again.

Mark sat alone for a moment, then he heard a buzzer sound further down the ward, followed by another – and another. The two nurses hurried past him, but neither saw him sitting silently in the darkness.

"That should keep them busy for a while!" hissed Archie as he appeared back at the wheelchair, then he pushed Mark out past the now-empty nurse's station, and into the hospital beyond.

The corridors were deserted. "What time is it?" asked Mark. He had forgotten to check the time on his PS Vita before leaving the ward.

"Two thirty-ish," said Archie, pushing the chair. "I couldn't sleep. I was too worried about tomorrow. What do you think happens?"

"In the operations?" said Mark. "I don't know. I don't trust Dr Stone, though."

"I spoke to Mr Denby, in the bed by the door," said Archie. "He's in for his third heart operation this year. He says Dr Stone is a great surgeon."

"Yes, but Mr Denby has a huge family who come in to see him every night," Mark pointed out. "So many that they have to borrow chairs from other patients. They'd soon kick up a fuss if he suddenly disappeared."

They reached the bank of lifts at the end of the corridor. Archie pressed the 'down' button. "Mr Denby said that Dr Stone's operating theatre isn't upstairs with the others. He has a new one the hospital built in the basement for him."

DING! The lift doors opened, forcing both boys to shield their eyes against the harsh light inside.

"Then I guess we're going down," said Mark.

They found the operating theatre easily. The doors weren't locked, so the pair crept inside. In the centre of the room, beneath a large inactive light, sat a vast operating table. Various machines and monitors – all switched off – crowded around the sides of the theatre. Archie parked Mark beside a trolley laid out with scalpels, clamps and other horrific-looking surgical tools.

"What are we looking for?" asked Archie, creeping around the room.

"I don't know," Mark admitted. "Something that looks out of place, I guess."

"OK," said Archie. "But how do we know what's out of place in an operating theatre? I've never been inside one before…"

Before Mark could reply, a light switched on in the room next door, sending a shaft of light shooting across the operating table. Mark ducked below the light and wheeled himself over to Archie, who was crouching behind some kind of monitor.

"Do they do operations at night?" Archie whispered.

Mark shrugged. "I guess they do if there's an emergency."

"It's Dr Stone!" said Archie, risking a glance at the window into the next room. Mark looked. The surgeon was wearing a green gown and mask, and was scrubbing his hands beneath a running tap.

"Then this definitely is an emergency!" hissed Mark. "We have to get out of here…"

Suddenly, the doors to the operating theatre crashed open and the hospital porter pushed a bed into the room. Lying on the bed, not moving, was a middle-aged woman. The porter lifted her onto the operating table.

Mark and Archie peered out from their hiding place.

"Who's that?" mouthed Archie, pointing to the figure on the table.

"I've no idea," Mark mouthed back. "She must be from the ward next to ours."

Lights blinked on and Dr Stone entered the room. He took a moment to study the woman on the operating table, then he turned to the porter. Miss Green's had the injection?

The porter nodded. "Yes sir, but…"

"But nothing!" spat Dr Stone. "You'll get your cut as usual. Now get out of here!"

Blinking hard, the porter pushed the bed out into the corridor outside, applied the brakes to keep it in place, then hurried away. Dr Stone turned back to his patient.

"Hello, Miss Green!" he soothed. "I'll be your surgeon for this evening…"

Mark and Archie watched in horror as Dr Stone chose a scalpel from his tray and got to work. But this wasn't any operation Mark had heard about before. Miss Green wasn't having pins inserted into a broken bone, or her appendix removed.

Instead… Mark swallowed hard. What he was seeing was almost too gruesome to bear…

Dr Stone cut the entire body into pieces!

Mark could feel Archie sobbing silently beside him. He put an arm around the boy's shoulders and hugged him tightly. This was something no one should ever have to witness – but there was worse to come.

Once Miss Green was nothing more than a pile of meat, the door to the operating theatre swung open and another figure appeared. It was an older woman with a broken-toothed smile that Mark recognised as the kitchen worker the nurses called Grotbags!

"How was she?" Grotbags asked, picking up a piece of arm and squeezing it.

"A little scared at first," replied Dr Stone from behind his mask. "In fact – she almost went to pieces!" The pair cackled together for a moment, then the surgeon's hard expression fell back over his eyes.

"You've got something for me?"

Grotbags nodded and pulled a thick stack of money from the pocket of her apron. "I still say this is too much."

"Do you want a supply of cheap meat for the kitchen or not?" Dr Stone snarled. "I have certain people to pay to keep their mouths shut."

Grotbags sighed and handed over the cash.

"Wonderful doing business with you!" said Dr Stone. "Any idea what you'll make of Miss Green?"

"I thought I could smell lasagne on Ward 13 tonight," said Grotbags, rummaging through the assorted body parts at the end of the table, "although I don't know why – I served chicken. Or, at least, what I told everyone was chicken." The woman lifted a severed foot to her nose and sniffed at it as though it was a prime cut of steak. "Yeah, I reckon she'd go lovely with a few layers of pasta!"

Mark couldn't help himself. That had been the writing on his piece of chicken earlier! R… O… Y… A… L… N… A… V… Y…

Jack's tattoo! He vomited – loudly.

CHAPTER 6

THE OPERATION

Dr Stone strode over to the monitors and peered over the top. "Who's there?" he demanded.

Mark wiped the sick from his pyjama top and turned to Archie. "Go!" he cried. "Run!"

"I can't leave you!"

"Run, now!"

Archie leaped up and pushed past Dr Stone. He raced for the door. Grotbags saw him coming and swung at him with the severed foot, but

Archie was fast. He quickly changed direction and dropped to the floor, sliding underneath the operating table and out the other side.

Grotbags chased him out of the operating theatre doors, but was back in a less than a minute, out of breath. "I couldn't… catch him…" she wheezed.

"Never mind the little one," growled Dr Stone, turning back to Mark. "I know where to find him. But this one…"

He reached down and grabbed Mark by the neck of his pyjamas, dragging him awkwardly to his feet. "This one has already been sticking his nose in where it doesn't belong. Perhaps it's time we stuck it somewhere else – like inside one of your meat pies!"

Grotbags hurried over to take hold of Mark's arm. Dr Stone released his grip on Mark and turned to collect something from his tray of implements. It was a large syringe, loaded with a green liquid.

"Say hello to my own little mixture of medicines…" the surgeon beamed. "I call it *Stone's stonemaker*…"

Mark struggled to get free. He swung up his fist, aiming for Grotbags's face, but she caught his wrist and forced it painfully back down to his side.

"You'll have to do better than that if you want to avoid ending up as someone's din-dins," she grinned.

"You won't get away with this!" Mark snapped.

"Oh, but I will," soothed Dr Stone. "Who's going to miss an annoying little runt like you? Certainly not the innocent shoppers you annoy with your skateboard antics down in the precinct every evening."

"There are the carers at Keating House!" said Mark. "They'll come looking for me."

Dr Stone laughed. "You won't be the first kid who's run away from his children's home," he said. "I'll simply tell them we found one of the windows open in the middle of the night – and your bed was empty. They'll call the police to look for you but, by that time, you'll be safely digested!"

"No!" cried Mark. "You can't…"

"Yes!" exclaimed Dr Stone. "I can!" Then he plunged the syringe into Mark's upper arm and injected the green liquid directly into the boy's veins.

The effect was almost instant. Mark found his muscles stiffening and his chest growing hard. He struggled to breathe and tried to raise a hand to his mouth – but found that he couldn't move.

"Wh… what's happening?" he croaked.

"*Stone's stonemaker!*" said Dr Stone as he and Grotbags lifted Mark onto the operating table. The metal surface felt cold against his back, but he couldn't do anything about it. He couldn't move at all. Even his eyes were locked in place, staring straight up at the blinding light.

The surgeon's face came into view. He sneered down at Mark. "Instant petrification! Good word, isn't it? It means you can no longer move any part of your body at all – not unless I inject you with the antidote, of course. And, the best part is – you're wide awake and can still feel pain."

Mark breathed fast, tears forming in the corners of his eyes.

"I usually finish my victims off first so they don't feel the agony of being dismembered – piece by piece – they just fall asleep and never wake up again. But, in your case, I think I'll make an exception…"

Laughing, Dr Stone placed the empty syringe onto his tray and selected a scalpel to begin his work. Mark watched the razor-sharp blade glint in the light as it came closer and closer to his face.

"Let's start with that pesky nose, shall we?"

Suddenly, the doors to the operating theatre crashed open.

Dr Stone spun round and shouted. "What are you lot doing here? Get back to work this instant!"

Mark couldn't turn his head to see who had entered the room, but he could see their reflection in the metal casing of the light above him. Standing in the doorway were half a dozen nurses, the hospital porter – and Archie!

Nurse Helen held up a syringe containing a red liquid. "The antidote to *Stone's stonemaker*!" she announced. "We found it in your locker."

Dr Stone laughed. "Too bad you don't have the courage to use it!" he spat.

The nurses glanced at one another nervously.

"I told you so," said Dr Stone. He turned to Grotbags. "Get them out of here…"

The bulky kitchen worker took a step forwards and the nurses began to back away. But the porter stood his ground.

"No," he said. "No more…"

He grabbed Grotbags by the wrist and twisted her arm up her back. The woman cried out in pain.

Archie turned to Helen. "Go on!" he urged the nurse. "Set Mark free!"

But Helen – and the other nurses – didn't move.

"He's not that scary!"

The nurses just stared at Dr Stone in terror.

Archie sighed. "If you want something doing…" he snatched the syringe from Helen's hand and raced across the operating theatre.

"Oh, no you don't!" bellowed Dr Stone. He threw his scalpel directly at Archie, the spinning blade just missing the boy's head, but nicking his ear and drawing blood.

"What a crap shot!" Archie yelled. He reached the table and stabbed the needle deep into Mark's thigh.

Mark felt his entire body begin to tingle. He found he could turn his head, and watched as Dr Stone grabbed another scalpel and lunged furiously at Archie. Mark cried out. He had to help his friend, but he couldn't jump off the table and fight because of his broken leg.

That was it! His broken leg!

Using all his effort as the antidote swept through his veins, Mark swung his broken leg out as hard as he could. The solid white plaster cast hit Dr Stone's jaw with an almighty CRACK! Then the surgeon slumped to the floor, out cold.

"*Stone's stonemaker!*" laughed Mark as Alfie helped him to sit upright. "It's nothing compared to Jackson's jawcracker!"

CHAPTER 7

THE REVENGE

Dr Stone woke groggily, forcing his eyes open against a thudding pain that completely enveloped his head – but seemed to be focussed on his jaw. He tried to raise a hand to rub his chin, but found he couldn't move.

"It's good stuff, this mixture of yours!" said a voice. "Works really quickly." A face came into view, then another. Dr Stone found himself looking up at Mark and Archie – and the younger boy was holding a syringe with the remains of a green liquid inside. A row of angry nurses stood behind the pair.

The surgeon tried to scream, but could only make a weak gurgling sound.

"Just to give you an update…" said Mark, smiling, "you're in Ward 13, and the police have been called. However, it's a busy night for them – what with them receiving dozens of anonymous calls reporting people missing tonight…"

Archie grinned. "I got to do a few of those!"

Mark nodded. "You know what we're like, us boys!" he beamed. "We get bored very easily so we go out skateboarding to try our hand at tricks and stunts…" He raised a finger as if an idea had just occurred to him. "Or… we could pass the time by playing 'Doctors and Nurses'. Yes, I think a bit of scalpel practice would be in order."

The nurse with the curly hair turned to the hospital porter. "Take him down to the operating theatre."

The porter nodded and began to push Dr Stone's bed towards the exit of Ward 13.

Squeak! Squeak! Squeak!

Out of the corner of his eye, the surgeon could see the kitchen worker lying on another of the empty beds, bound and gagged.

Mark half limped, half hopped to catch up with the bed as it was wheeled out into the corridor.

"Can you hear the sirens yet?" he asked Dr Stone. "No, me neither – at least not over the sound of that squeaky wheel."

SQUEAK! SQUEAK! SQUEAK!

"I wonder if the police will get here before we reach the operating theatre…" Mark continued.

SQUEAK! SQUEAK! SQUEAK!

"If not – I hope they're hungry!"

THE END